SLEEPYHEADS

Sandra J. Howatt

illustrated by Joyce Wan

Beach Lane Books
New York London Toronto Sydney New Delhi

See the moon? It's sleepy time.
Let's look for little beds
and find where all the little ones
lay their sleepy heads.

Look! I see a sleepyhead
cuddled in a nest.

I see another sleepyhead
who thinks a hole is best.

Look! I see a sleepyhead
nestled in a cave.

I see another sleepyhead
rocking on a wave.

Look! I see a sleepyhead
snuggled in the reeds.

I see another sleepyhead
resting in the weeds.

Look! I see a sleepyhead
burrowed in the hay.

This one's not a sleepyhead—
this one slept all day!

See the house? Let's peek inside.
Let's look for little beds
and find where all the little ones
lay their sleepy heads.

Look! I see a sleepyhead
beside the fireplace.

I see another sleepyhead
curled tight in its dark space.

Look! I see a teddy bear,
a pillow, and a bed.

I see a blanket, soft and warm.
But where's the sleepyhead?

We found all the little ones
in trees, in holes, in caves.

We found all the sleepyheads
in weeds, in reeds, on waves.

We found all but one small one
in houses and in barns.

Where is that little sleepyhead?

Asleep in Mama's arms!

For my beautiful sleepyheads, Amy, Katy, and Sarah;
and their sleepyheads, Andrew, Nicholas, Kayleigh,
Alexander, Zachary, Aidyn, and Kaylin.
And, of course, for my mama
—S. J. H.

For Steve—J. W.

 BEACH LANE BOOKS • An imprint of Simon & Schuster Children's Publishing Division • 1230 Avenue of the Americas, New York, New York 10020 • Text copyright © 2014 by Sandra Howatt • Illustrations copyright © 2014 by Joyce Wan • All rights reserved, including the right of reproduction in whole or in part in any form. • BEACH LANE BOOKS is a trademark of Simon & Schuster, Inc. • For information about special discounts for bulk purchases, please contact Simon & Schuster Special Sales at 1-866-506-1949 or business@simonandschuster.com. • The Simon & Schuster Speakers Bureau can bring authors to your live event. For more information or to book an event, contact the Simon & Schuster Speakers Bureau at 1-866-248-3049 or visit our website at www.simonspeakers.com. • Book design by Lauren Rille • The text for this book is set in Amasis. • The illustrations for this book are rendered in pencil and then colored digitally. • Manufactured in China • 0214 SCP • First Edition • 10 9 8 7 6 5 4 3 2 1 • Library of Congress Cataloging-in-Publication Data • Howatt, Sandra J • Sleepyheads / by Sandra J. Howatt ; illustrated by Joyce Wan.—First edition. • p. cm. • Summary: "Drowsy animal babies snuggle in trees, caves, weeds, and on waves, but one sleepyhead isn't yet in his bed"—Provided by publisher. • ISBN 978-1-4424-2266-7 (hardcover) • ISBN 978-1-4424-4678-6 (eBook) • [1. Stories in rhyme. 2. Bedtime—Fiction. 3. Sleep—Fiction. 4. Babies—Fiction. 5. Animals—Sleep behavior—Fiction. 6. Animals—Infancy—Fiction.] I. Wan, Joyce, illustrator. II. Title. PZ8.3.H8375Sl 2014 • [E]—dc23 • 2013013607